W9-BWH-835

By Wanda Coven
Illustrated by Priscilla Burris

LITTLE SIMON
New York London Toronto Sydney New Delhi

If you purchased this book without a cover, you should be aware that this book is stolen property. It was reported as "unsold and destroyed" to the publisher, and neither the author nor the publisher has received any payment for this "stripped book."

This book is a work of fiction. Any references to historical events, real people, or real places are used fictitiously. Other names, characters, places, and events are products of the author's imagination, and any resemblance to actual events or places or persons, living or dead, is entirely coincidental.

LITTLE SIMON
An imprint of Simon & Schuster Children's Publishing Division
1230 Avenue of the Americas, New York, New York 10020
First Little Simon paperback edition January 2017

Also available in a Little Simon hardcover edition.

Designed by Ciara Gay
Manufactured in the United States of America 1216 MTN
10 9 8 7 6 5 4 3 2 1
Library of Congress Cataloging-in-Publication Data
Names: Coven, Wanda, author. | Burris, Priscilla, illustrator.
Title: Heidi Heckelbeck tries out for the team / by Wanda Coven ; illustrated by Priscilla Burris. | Description: First Little Simon paperback edition. | New York : Little Simon, 2017. | Series: Heidi Heckelbeck ; #19 | Summary: After trying unsuccessfully to play a variety of school sports, Heidi turns to the *Book of Spells*. | Identifiers: LCCN 2016016200 | ISBN 9781481471725 (pbk) | ISBN 9781481471732 (hc) | ISBN 9781481471749 (eBook)
Subjects: | CYAC: Sports—Fiction. | Schools—Fiction. | Magic—Fiction. | Witches—Fiction. | BISAC: JUVENILE FICTION / Readers / Chapter Books. | JUVENILE FICTION / Fantasy & Magic. | JUVENILE FICTION / Imagination & Play. | Classification: LCC PZ7.C83393 Hn 2017 | DDC [Fic]—dc23 LC record available at https://lccn.loc.gov/2016016200

CONTENTS

Run!
Kick!
Jump!

GET MOVING!

Dribble!

Dribble!

Shoot!

Score!

Sporty cardboard signs dangled from the gym ceiling. Each one had something written on it in fat, colorful

GET MOVING!
Dribble! Dribble!
Run!
Kick!
Jump!
BATTER UP!
SCORE!

letters: RUN!, KICK!, JUMP!, and BATTER UP! There was even a banner on the wall behind the bleachers that said GET MOVING! Tables with ruffled skirts stood all around the gym. Each table had a poster with a different sport on it: SOCCER, BASEBALL, VOLLEYBALL, BASKETBALL, TRACK AND FIELD, and CHEERLEADING.

"What's up with all the sports stuff?" Heidi asked.

Lucy Lancaster shrugged and nudged Bruce Bickerson. "Do you know?"

"Looks like a sports fair," Bruce said as they climbed the bleachers

and sat with the rest of the students.

Principal Pennypacker stood in front of the school with a microphone. "Good morning, Brewster sports fans!" he said as he smoothed one of the tufts of hair on the side of his head.

"Good morning!" the students responded.

The principal motioned toward the tables. "Who likes sports?" he asked.

The students clapped and hooted their approval. Everyone except Heidi. She didn't dislike sports, but they had never really been her thing. She waited to hear more.

"Today we kick off our new after-school sports program," he explained. "Everyone gets to pick a sport and

try it out." Then he explained how to sign up at one of the tables.

The bleachers creaked and moaned as the kids hurried down to the tables to sign up.

"What sport are you going to play, Heidi?" asked Lucy.

Heidi nibbled the back of her thumb uncertainly. She had never played on a real sports team before other than in Coach Wardner's gym class. "I dunno," she said. "What about you?"

Lucy looked at the tables. "I'd like to try soccer," she said. "I love to run, dribble the ball, and score goals. Sometimes I do it for fun in my backyard."

Heidi nodded. "How about you, Bruce?" she asked.

"Baseball," Bruce said, pretending to swing a bat. "I like the science of it."

Lucy blinked in surprise. "Since when is baseball a science?" she questioned.

Bruce laughed. "Everything about baseball is scientific," he said. "From how fast the ball goes when you hit it, to how much spin you get when the ball is pitched. Not to mention the math behind batting averages and on-base statistics!"

"Wow," Lucy said. "I had no idea."

Bruce and Lucy chatted away as they walked to the sign-up tables.

"Come on, Heidi!" called Lucy over her shoulder.

But Heidi stayed put. She had no idea what sport she wanted to try. She didn't even know if she wanted to try one at all. Then someone tapped her on the shoulder. It was Principal Pennypacker.

"Need help picking a sport?" he asked cheerfully.

Heidi's eyes looked away. "Nah, see, I'm not really the sporty type," she muttered.

Principal Pennypacker laughed. "You can't fool me, Heidi Heckelbeck!" he said. "I know you play a mean game of four square."

Heidi sighed. "That's different," she said. "Besides, what if I stink at sports?"

The principal shrugged. "Then pick another!" he suggested.

Heidi raised an eyebrow. “You mean I can sign up for more than one?”

The principal smiled. “Why don’t you sign up for as many as you’d like?” he said. “That will be our special deal.”

Heidi liked special deals. So she got in line behind Lucy and signed up for soccer first. If Lucy liked it, then Heidi was sure she’d like it too.

FALLiNG SOCCER STAR

Uh-oh, Heidi said to herself as she jogged onto the soccer field after school the next day. *Everyone has on shorts and soccer cleats.* Heidi had on a skirt and tights. She elbowed Lucy.

"Why didn't you tell me we had to wear special clothes?" she asked.

Lucy looked Heidi up and down. “Um, oopsies,” she said. “I thought you knew!”

Heidi tried to cover her outfit with her arms. “This is just SO embarrassing,” she whispered.

“Hey, don’t worry,” said Lucy. “You’ll just wear shorts next time.”

Then Mrs. Noddywonks blew her

whistle. Mrs. Noddywonks was the drama teacher, but now she was also coaching after-school soccer. Even *she* had on workout clothes.

"Time for warm-ups!" the coach said, emptying a bag of soccer balls onto the grass. "Everyone grab a ball!"

Heidi and Lucy each grabbed a pink soccer ball.

"Now pretend the ball is your paint-roller," said Mrs. Noddywonks. "Wherever the ball rolls, imagine it's painting the field. Begin by painting a circle. Then try a square and a triangle."

Lucy dropped her ball and dribbled it in a great big circle. Heidi did the same. Then she did a square.

“This isn’t so bad,” Heidi said.

“Told you,” Lucy said, completing a triangle.

Then Mrs. Noddywonks had them paint their names with the ball. Heidi dribbled an *H*, but it got too twisty and turny. She stumbled over her ball

and fell to her knees. She looked at her tights. She had grass stains on both knees.

Lucy reached out her hand. "There's a lot of falling in soccer," she said. "It's the players who get back up who succeed."

Heidi frowned and grabbed hold of Lucy's hand.

Next they practiced passing. Heidi kicked the ball to Lucy. Lucy faked left, then right, before she passed the ball back. Lucy had all kinds of fancy moves. Heidi had none.

Then Mrs. Noddywonks picked teams. She put Heidi and Lucy on opposite sides. The whistle blew. Lucy got the ball and dribbled toward Heidi. Heidi tried to stop her, but Lucy faked and dribbled right by her.

Heidi spun around to go after Lucy, but she slipped and landed on her hands and knees. More grass stains. Then the ball came back up the field. Heidi kicked it and landed right on her rump.

The rest of the practice did not go better for Heidi. She spent most of the time on the ground.

Finally, Mrs. Noddywonks blew the last whistle. "Gym clothes next time," she said to Heidi.

Heidi looked at her grass-stained outfit. *If there is a next time,* she said to herself.

BACKWARD BASEBALL!

"How'd you like soccer?" asked Lucy.

Heidi slurped a noodle from her chicken noodle soup. "It was okay," she said.

Bruce leaned over and plucked a piece of grass from Heidi's hair. "Look what I found!" he said with a laugh.

"Ew!" Heidi said, grabbing it from his hand. "I thought I'd washed it all out last night." She wrapped the piece of grass in her napkin.

Then Melanie Maplethorpe stood in front of their table. She had signed up for the cheerleading squad and was wearing a pink-and-white uniform. Melanie smiled and began to perform a little cheer:

"Look at Heidi
kick the ball!
Look at Heidi
take a fall!
Brush that mud
right off
your bum,
before it sticks
like chewing gum!"

The whole cafeteria burst into laughter.

Heidi slid down in her seat.

"Just *ignore* her," Lucy said firmly. "That girl is beastly."

Heidi sat up a little. *Totally beastly,* she repeated to herself.

"So I have an idea," said Bruce, changing the subject. "Why don't you try baseball with me instead? Our coach is Mr. Doodlebee."

Heidi liked Mr. Doodlebee—or Mr. Doodlebug, as she liked to call him. Plus she had swung a bat a few times at a cookout.

"Okay," Heidi agreed. "I'll give it a try."

That afternoon on the baseball field, Heidi wiggled her fingers into a glove and played catch with Bruce.

She opened her glove to catch the ball. *Thunk!* It landed on the ground in front of her. She picked it up and threw it back to Bruce. Then he threw her a grounder. Heidi lined her glove

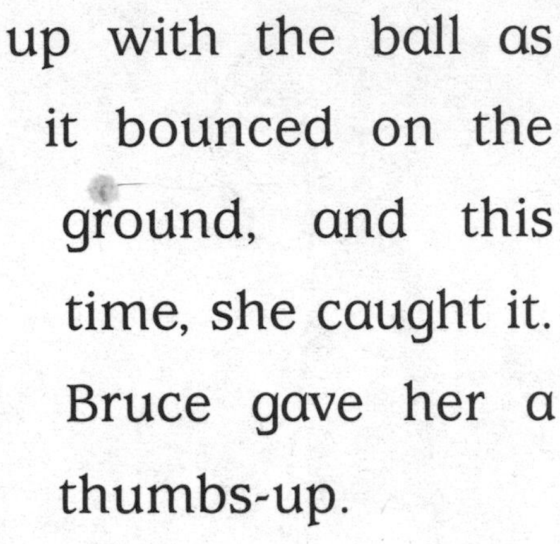

up with the ball as it bounced on the ground, and this time, she caught it. Bruce gave her a thumbs-up.

Then they played a game. Mr. Doodlebee asked Heidi to bat first. *Oh, gulp,* Heidi thought. *Why do I have to be FIRST?* She put on a helmet, picked up a bat, and walked to home plate. She looked at the pitcher. He pitched the ball, and it whizzed right by her!

The umpire said, "Strike one!"

Heidi had no time to think. The pitcher wound up and threw another ball. This time she swung the bat as hard as she could. *Whoosh!* She hit nothing but air.

"Str-r-r-ike TWO!" announced the umpire.

Heidi looked at the plate.

"You can DO IT!" Bruce shouted.

Heidi lifted the bat. She squinted and bent her back slightly. Again, the ball whizzed toward her. She swung the bat. And *CRACK!* This time she hit the ball! It flew right past an outfielder.

"RUN!" everyone shouted. "Run to first base!"

Heidi took off running. She ran around *all* the bases. Everyone stared at Heidi in disbelief.

"I got a home run!" she cried happily as she crossed home plate.

But Mr. Doodlebee didn't look very excited.

"Well, not exactly," he said.

Heidi's face fell. "But I ran all the bases," she said.

"Yes, you did," Mr. Doodlebee agreed. "You ran all the bases in *reverse*."

Heidi heard some of the kids snicker. She pulled her helmet down to hide her eyes and slinked off the field. Maybe baseball wasn't her sport after all?

ALL TANGLED UP

The next day Melanie performed another cheer for Heidi:

"Heidi! Heidi! Yo! Ho! Ho!
She's a crazy baseball pro!
She runs the bases in reverse!
On the team, there's no one worse!
Go, Heidi!"

Heidi rolled her eyes and shook her head.

"Didn't you like my cheer?" Melanie asked innocently.

Heidi rushed past Melanie into the classroom. Laurel Lambert ran to catch up with Heidi.

"Don't let Smell-a-nie bother you,"

Laurel said. "That's how she wants you to feel."

"Well, she got what she wanted," Heidi said angrily, dropping her backpack onto the floor with a thud.

Laurel stuffed her backpack into her cubby. "That girl is major-league annoying. Everyone knows it."

Heidi smiled ever so slightly. She felt a little better knowing that other people might feel the same way about Melanie.

"So how did you like baseball?" asked Laurel. "Not counting the part about running the bases backward."

Heidi frowned. "Well, catching the ball is pretty fun," she said. "Batting is too, especially when you hit the ball."

The girls sat down at their desks.

"Then maybe you would like volleyball,"

Laurel suggested. “If you can catch and hit in baseball, you might be good at volleyball.”

Heidi unzipped her pencil case. “I’ll try it on one condition,” she said.

"You have to explain the rules to me BEFORE I get on the court."

"I promise," Laurel said.

The volleyball team met in the gym, and her teacher Mrs. Welli was the coach. Laurel explained the rules and

showed Heidi how to clasp her hands to hit the ball. Then everyone volleyed the balls back and forth.

Heidi bumped a ball, but it landed on the same side she was standing on. She knocked another ball out of bounds. Then Heidi whomped one over the net. *That felt pretty good,* she said to herself. Then they practiced under-hand serves.

Mrs. Welli blew her whistle. "Let's try a game," she said.

Everybody moved in position. Heidi stood in the front row while Laurel was in the back row. The other team served the ball first. Laurel bumped it to Heidi. Heidi's sneakers squeaked as she got under the ball. She hit it over the net. Mrs. Welli blew the whistle again.

"We got a point!" Heidi shouted. She high-fived Laurel. Things were going well.

Then it was Heidi's turn to serve. She lifted the ball and punched it from underneath. *SMACK!* The ball hit Laurel right in the back. Laurel yelped.

Heidi cupped her hand over her mouth.

"SORRY!" she cried.

Laurel arched her back to shake off the sting.

Now it was the other team's turn. They served the ball to Heidi. She ran toward it as it dropped. Heidi dove for the ball, but it was going straight into the

net. Heidi tried to stop in time, but she was too late. The ball, the net, and Heidi tumbled to the ground. Everyone gasped.

Mrs. Welli blew the whistle.

Heidi felt like a fish caught in net. And fish don't play volleyball.

ON THE RiGHT TRACK

Heidi sat on her front steps, thinking. She noticed Stanley Stonewrecker walking down the sidewalk.

"Hey, Heidi!" he called.

Heidi waved back halfheartedly.

"What's the matter?" he asked.

Heidi shrugged. "I stink at sports."

Stanley dropped his backpack and plunked down next to Heidi. "Which sports?" he asked.

Heidi held out her fingers and counted. "You name it. I stink at soccer, I double-stink at baseball, and I triple-stink at volleyball."

Stanley chuckled.

"I'm SERIOUS!" Heidi said. She shoved Stanley with her shoulder. He swayed to one side.

"Okay, so don't play sports you stink at," he said. "Try a new one."

"I'll probably stink at that, too," Heidi said, and she pushed out her lower lip into a pout.

Stanley smiled. "Are you good at running?" he asked.

"Pretty good," Heidi answered.

"What about jumping and throwing?"

"Not bad," Heidi said.

"Then why not try track with me?"

Heidi thought

about it. *Maybe a sport that doesn't involve a BALL is just what I need.*

The next day Heidi showed up for track. Principal Pennypacker was the coach. He wore a tracksuit and a purple sweatband on his nearly bald head. He waved Heidi over.

“Come warm up with us!” he called.

Heidi joined the group of kids and stood next to Stanley. She followed the principal’s stretching workout closely. She swirled her hips in a circle ten times. She did lunges and

jumping jacks. Then the team lined up at the edge of the field.

"When I say 'Go,' run as fast as you can to the orange cones," the principal directed. "On your mark! Get set! Go!"

Heidi took off like a rocket and ran her fastest across the field. She crossed the finish line in the middle of the pack. She bent over to catch her breath. *I did pretty well!* she said to herself.

Heidi tried the long jump next. She dashed to the takeoff board and leaped into the air. *Whump!* she landed awkwardly in the sandpit and rolled over. She spit some sand out of her mouth.

"Nice first jump, Heidi!" Principal Pennypacker cheered her on. "Let's see another!"

Heidi jogged back to the top of the runway.

"Don't overthink it," said the principal. "Just run and jump."

Heidi tried again. This time she landed better.

Principal Pennypacker clapped his hands. "You're a natural!" he shouted.

Heidi smiled and then brushed the sand off her hands onto her shorts.

Then she watched Stanley leap hurdles. He cleared all ten.

Heidi loved to jump over things. *This should be a cinch!* she said to herself.

She lined up. Principal Pennypacker blew the whistle, and Heidi sprinted toward the hurdles. *Bam!* She knocked down the first one. *Bam! Bam! Bam!* She knocked down two, three, and four. Then she tripped over hurdle five and face-planted in the grass.

Stanley ran to Heidi's side. "Are you okay?" he whispered.

Heidi moaned. "No, I'm dying of embarrassment." Then she got up, limped off the field, and headed for home.

UNDERCOVER

Heidi wore dark glasses and a hat to school the next day. She waited until everyone was seated and tiptoed to her desk. Mrs. Welli took attendance.

"Lucy Lancaster?"

"Here!"

"Bruce Bickerson?"

"Here."

"Heidi Heckelbeck?"

Heidi just head-bobbed.

She barely said a word all day. If someone asked her a question, she gave a quick, short answer.

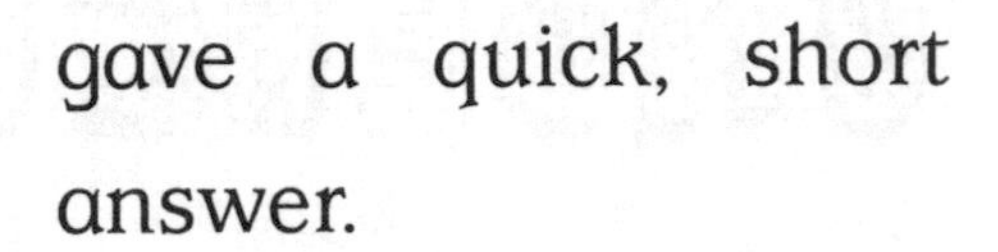

"What's up with the disguise?" asked Lucy.

"Dirty hair," Heidi said.

She also dodged everyone. In art she sat on the last stool at the table against the

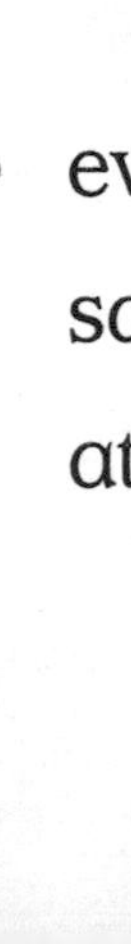

wall. In math, reading, and science, she leaned on her elbows and let her hair fall like a curtain on either side of her face. She didn't raise her hand once—even when she knew the answers. Heidi spent recess and lunch in the library.

When the final bell rang, Heidi waited in the girls' room until everyone had left for the day. Then she made a run for the bus. At the bottom of the stairs, she ran into Melanie. Melanie had been waiting for Heidi.

"THERE you are!" she said.

Heidi froze in horror as Melanie began one of her loud, annoying cheers:

"Heidi! Heidi!
Sis boom bah!
Trips those
hurdles!
Rah! Rah! Rah!"

This time something inside Heidi snapped. She walked right up to Melanie's super-cheerleader face.

"You know what?" Heidi said with

a little snip in her voice. "You just gave me a GREAT idea."

Melanie planted her hands on her hips and sniffed. "So, what's your BIG idea?"

Heidi folded her arms. "I, Heidi Heckelbeck, am going to join the CHEERLEADERS," she declared. "And YOU can't stop me."

Melanie laughed dramatically. "NO WAY. YOU?" she questioned. "A cheerleader? Ha! That's a GOOD one!"

Heidi glared at Melanie.

But Melanie shrugged her off. "Seriously, Heidi," she went on, "you just don't have the magic touch to be a cheerleader."

Heidi smiled devilishly. "Oh, we'll see about THAT," she said.

POM-POMS AND POOL WATER

Heidi whipped out her *Book of Spells* and opened it to the chapter on sports. She found one called the MVP Spell. *"MVP" means "most valuable player,"* Heidi said to herself. *That's exactly what I need!* She flipped to it and read over the spell.

The MVP Spell

Have you ever gone out for a sports team and had a bad tryout? Are you the kind of witch who can't seem to dribble, bat, spike, or score? If you feel like a spaz when it comes to anything athletic, then this is the spell for YOU!

Ingredients:

3 blades of soccer field grass

1 handful of home plate dirt

1 drop of swimming pool water

1 pom-pom

Mix the ingredients together in a bowl. Hold your Witches of Westwick medallion over your heart and place your other hand over the mix. Chant the following spell:

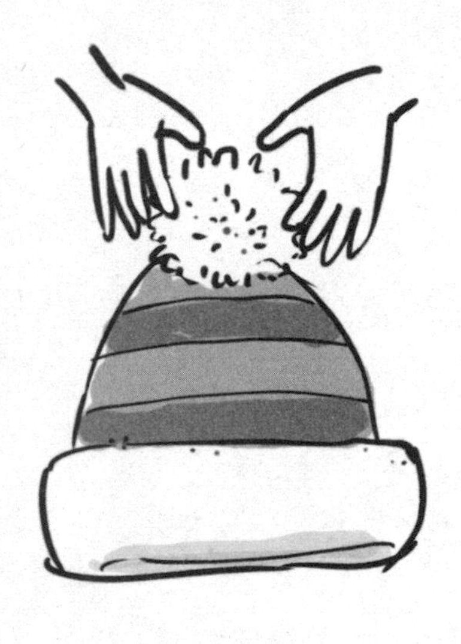

Heidi hunted for the correct magical ingredients early Saturday morning. First she snipped a pom-pom off an old ski hat. *No one will miss it,* she thought. Then she hopped on her scooter and rode to the park. She crept onto the baseball diamond and scooped a fistful of dirt from near home plate. She dumped it into a snack bag. Then she snuck onto the soccer field and plucked three blades of grass. *One more ingredient to go,* she said to herself.

Heidi scootered to the indoor pool and quietly entered the pool area. A blast of warm, steamy air washed over her. Voices echoed and water splashed as the swimmers practiced all their strokes. Heidi pulled out a small eyedropper from her backpack. She took a deep breath and hurried to the edge of the pool. She squeezed the rubber bulb on the top of the eyedropper and drew in some water.

A girl in a blue bathing cap popped out of the water like a seal. She surprised Heidi. "Whatcha doing?" she asked.

Heidi shoved the eyedropper quickly into her backpack. "Uh, science experiment," she blurted out. "About science stuff."

The girl rested her arm on the edge of the pool. "Oh," she said. "Do you go to Brewster?"

Heidi didn't dare answer. What if this girl said something about Heidi taking water from the pool? What if she got in trouble? Heidi backed away.

"Gotta go!" Heidi said. Then she dashed out the door and scootered home.

She put the magical ingredients in her desk drawer for safekeeping. Then a smile swept over her face. "I cannot wait to see the look on Smell-a-nie's face when I cheer!"

UNSTOPPABLE

On Monday afternoon, Heidi ducked under the bleachers to cast her MVP spell. She pulled a small bowl from her backpack and squeezed a drop of swimming pool water into it. *Plink!* She added the three blades of soccer field grass, the handful of dirt, and the pom-pom. She held her medallion over her heart with one hand and held her other hand over the mix. Then Heidi quietly chanted the spell.

"Swing, batter! Swing, batter!

Run! Shoot! Score!

MVP! MVP!

The fans all roar!"

Zap! A surge of energy raced through Heidi's body. *Whoa!* she said to her-self. *I feel like I could do ANYTHING!*

Then she burst out from behind the bleachers and cartwheeled across the lawn to the cheerleaders. She grabbed a set of pom-poms and tapped Melanie on the shoulder.

Melanie turned around and scowled at Heidi.

"I'm ready!" Heidi said cheerfully. She had to jog in place because her body wanted to go, go, *GO!*

"Do you even *know* a routine?" asked Melanie.

Heidi had studied all the cheer

moves the night before, so she knew exactly what to do. The spell would take care of the rest.

“Ready when you are!” Heidi said.

“Okay,” said Melanie with a snicker. “Feel free to completely embarrass yourself anytime.”

The other cheerleaders watched

Heidi to see what would happen.

Heidi got into position. "Five, six, seven, eight!" she counted.

Then Heidi did a spread-eagle jump, a toe touch, a Herkie, and a pike. She pointed her toes on every stunt and got great height. She even had a smile on her face the whole time.

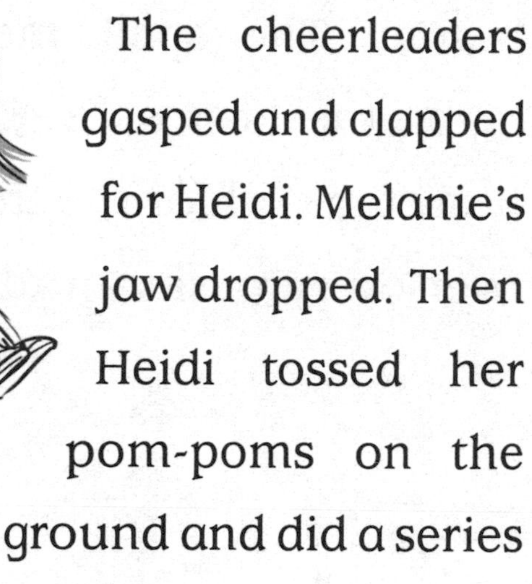

The cheerleaders gasped and clapped for Heidi. Melanie's jaw dropped. Then Heidi tossed her pom-poms on the ground and did a series of back handsprings across the field and walkovers all the way back. *Look at me! I'm amazing!* she said to herself. *I am completely UNSTOPPABLE!*

And it was true. Heidi had no off button. The spell made her want to be the best at *EVERYTHING*! Her body took off for the track. She sailed over every pesky hurdle. Then Heidi

sprinted to the long jump and cleared the entire sandpit.

Look out, baseball diamond! Here I come! she said to herself. Heidi

charged onto the field. She caught a fly ball, tagged a base runner, and then she threw another player out—it was a *triple play*!

Everyone cheered for Heidi, the sports star, as she zoomed over to the soccer field. *Oh no!* she cried to herself. *Here I go AGAIN!* Heidi snagged the ball in play and dribbled it down the field.

All the players were totally confused, but that didn't stop Heidi. She raced to the goal and kicked the ball with all her might. The goalie dove and missed as the soccer ball smacked against the back of the net. *GOAL!!!*

Then Heidi bolted into the gym. She rushed right onto the volleyball court and spiked the ball as it came over the net. *Wham!* Heidi got the game-winning point! Then she fell to floor and rolled over flat on her back.

Principal Pennypacker, who had been chasing her the entire time, blew his whistle. Then he helped Heidi to her feet. Together, they walked to his office and called her mother.

She could hear all the kids outside chanting, *"MVP! MVP! MVP!"*

Heidi buried her face in her hands. *I'm not the MVP,* she said to herself. *I'm the MRP. The Most Ridiculous Player.*

MIA

Mom sat on the couch next to Heidi.

"Okay, so what happened?" Mom asked gently. "Did it involve witching skills?"

Heidi slumped her shoulders and nodded. "I just wanted to be good at one silly sport," she mumbled. "But the spell made me great at all of them."

Mom put her arm around Heidi. "Sometimes magic can complicate problems rather than solving them. Did you find a sport you like?"

Heidi shook her head.

"Well, who knows? Maybe next time a sport will find you," Mom said.

Heidi's stomach growled. "Right now I want some food to find me. Playing five sports in one day can make a kid hungry."

They both laughed and went to the kitchen to make a snack.

The next day at recess Heidi stood in the four square line. A girl tapped Heidi on the shoulder. She turned to see the girl from the pool the other day.

"I knew we went to the same school," the girl said. "I'm Mia Marshall. I'm in third grade."

Heidi stepped forward in line. "I'm Heidi," she said.

Mia smiled. "I know, Ms. MVP," she said with a twinkle in her eye. "Your super sports stunts have made you famous at Brewster."

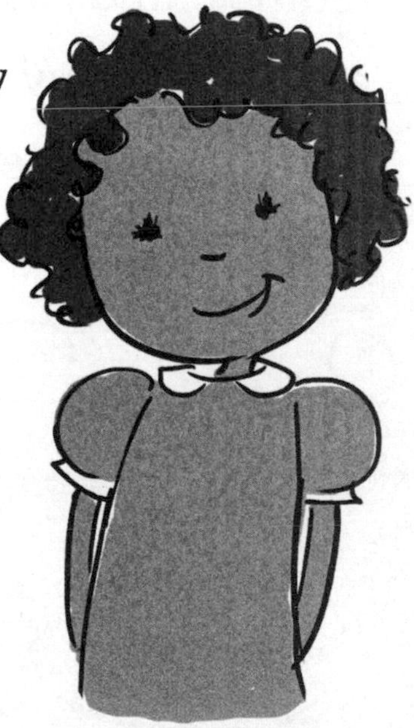

Heidi's cheeks grew warm. "That was kind of a crazy day for me," she admitted. "Believe it or not, I'm not really into any of those sports."

Mia nodded. "Same

here," she said. "That's why I tried swimming. Do you like to swim?"

Heidi nodded. "We go to the pool all the time in summer."

"Maybe you should join the swim team," Mia suggested. "We swim every Saturday. It's really fun."

Heidi had never thought of swim team. She laughed because it made

so much sense. Heidi had always loved the pool.

"Thanks, Mia," she said. "Maybe I will sign up."

EAT
MY
BUBBLES

THE LITTLE MERMAIDS

Heidi joined the Little Mermaids swim team on Saturday. She got a navy-blue swim suit with hot-pink stripes down the sides, along with a matching swim cap and goggles. She even got a T-shirt that said EAT MY BUBBLES on the back.

The team had its first swim meet at

the end of the month. Heidi spent the next few weeks training. Mia and the team's coach, Ms. Poole, helped her

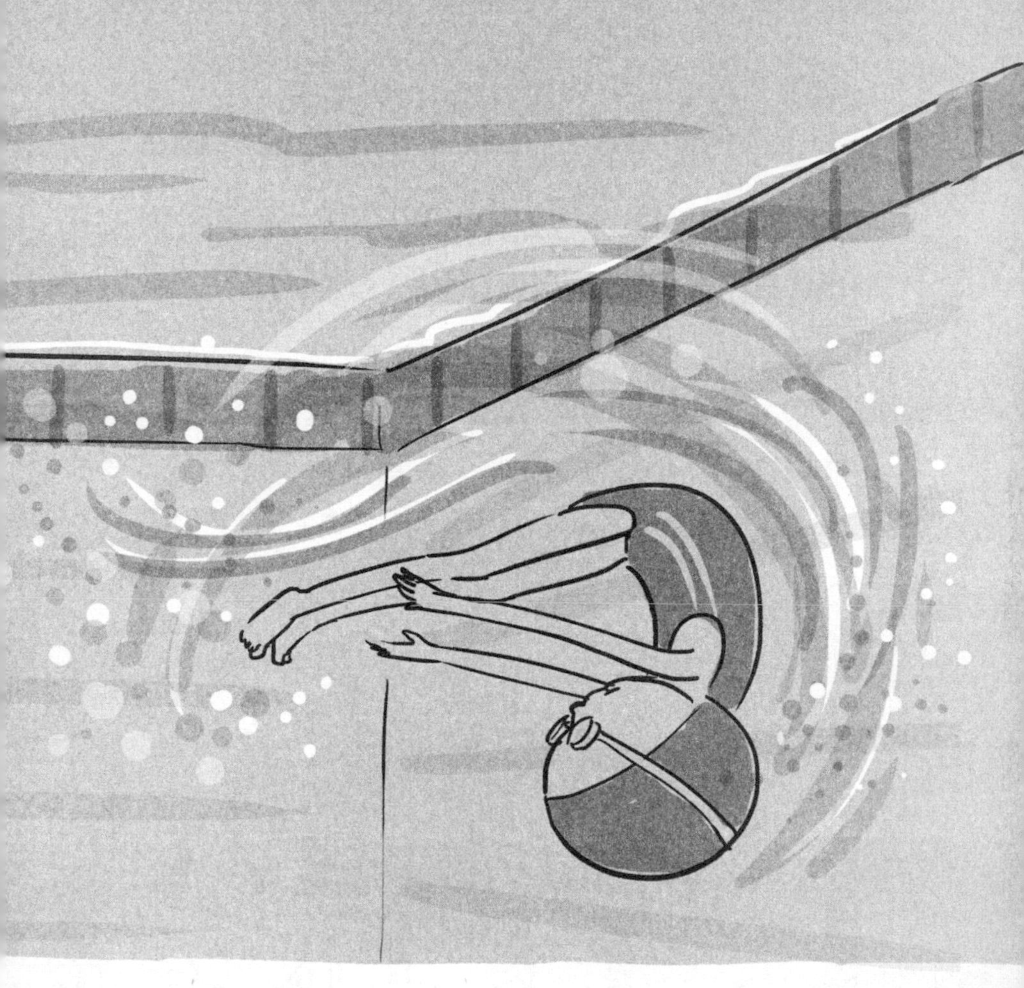

learn all the strokes. She even learned how to dive and do a flip turn against the pool wall.

When it was finally time for the swim meet, Heidi's whole family, including Aunt Trudy, sat in the bleachers to watch.

Heidi and the rest of the swimmers in the freestyle event stood on the starting blocks. Heidi tensed her stomach muscles to scare away the jitters.

"Hello and welcome, everyone, to the first swim meet of the year," said the announcer into his megaphone. "We'll *kick* this off with the Little Mermaids versus the Dolphins."

He turned toward the swimmers. "Swimmers, take your marks!"

Then he the blew whistle. *Splash!* The swimmers dove into their lanes.

Heidi circled her arms perfectly and flutter kicked across the pool.

The cool silkiness of the water washed over her back as she moved through the water. She listened to the splashing around her and the cheers from the stands.

Heidi flip turned and swam hard to the other end of the pool. She touched

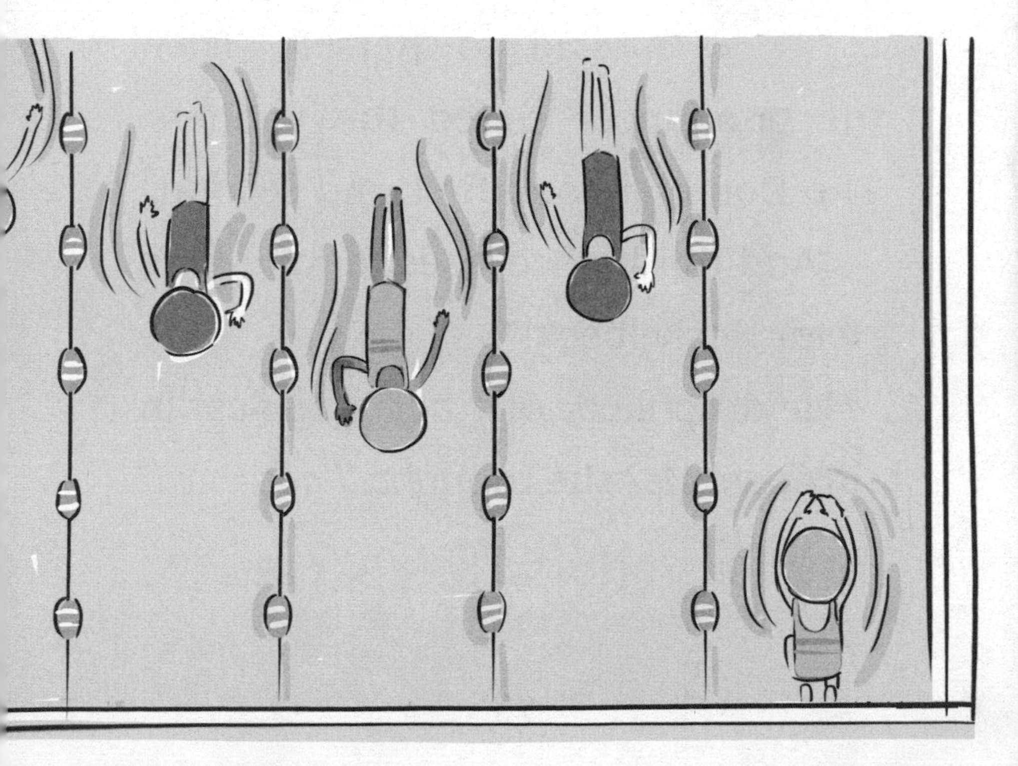

the wall and held on to the ledge with one hand. Other swimmers finished after her. *Well, at least I'm not LAST,* she said to herself. Then the announcer called the winners. The Dolphins took first and second.

"And third place goes to lane four, Heidi Heckelbeck!"

Heidi pulled off her goggles in surprise. *Me?* she thought. *I got third? No way!*

The winners stood on a platform in front of the bleachers. Then the coach handed out ribbons. She gave Heidi a yellow one.

Everyone clapped and cheered for Heidi.

Heidi waved proudly. *And the best part is that I did it ALL BY MYSELF,* she thought. *Not one speck of magic!*

Then she smiled. *Not that there's anything wrong with a little magic—sometimes.*

Skippity skip!

Hoppity hop!

Jumpity jump!

Heidi Heckelbeck, Lucy Lancaster, and Bruce Bickerson pranced along the path through Charmed Court Park. Bruce twirled a white Frisbee on the end of his pointer finger. Lucy hopped out of the way of two rollerbladers.

An excerpt from *Heidi Heckelbeck and the Magic Puppy*

Heidi stopped and pointed to a yoga class on the lawn.

"Let's see if we can do some of their poses!" she suggested.

They watched the yoga instructor. Lucy bent over into a dolphin pose. Bruce wove himself into an eagle pose. And Heidi struck a lord of the dance pose. Then they dropped to the ground, laughing.

"Now let's play on the giant chess-board!" Lucy said, taking off. Heidi and Bruce followed close behind. They played hide-and-seek among the oversize chess pieces. Then they ran to the playground, slid down the slides, and swung on the monkey bars.

"Let's ride the zip line!" cried Heidi.

Heidi climbed the curved ladder that led up to the wooden platform. Then she grabbed the cable and hopped onto the seat. The wire made a pleasing hum as she sailed through the air. She stuck out her feet, scrunched her knees, and pushed off the platform at the other end of the zip line, and back she went. Then Lucy and Bruce each had a turn.

An excerpt from *Heidi Heckelbeck and the Magic Puppy*